For Michael

*The half of this book—
the whole of my heart.*

A Dedication

She lends her pen,
    to thoughts of him,
    that flow from it,
    in her solitary.

For she is his poet,
    And he is her poetry.

Part 1
MISADVENTURE

A Toast!

To new beginnings,
    in fear and faith
    and all it tinges.

To love is a dare,
    when hope and despair,
    are gates upon it hinges.

Xs and Os

Love is a game
  of tic-tac-toe,
    constantly waiting,
    for the next x or o.

A DANGEROUS RECIPE

To love him
    is something,
    I hold highly
    suspicious.

Like having something,
    so very delicious—
    then being told,
    to do the dishes.

Just Friends

I know that I don't own you,
    and perhaps I never will,
    so my anger when you're with her,
    I have no right to feel.

I know that you don't owe me,
    and I shouldn't ask for more;
    I shouldn't feel so let down,
    all the times when you don't call.

What I feel—I shouldn't show you,
    so when you're around I won't;
    I know I've no right to feel it—
    but it doesn't mean I don't.

When Ignorance Is Bliss

I deplore,
    being ignored.

For—

I am not a bore!

But it's perplexingly sweet,
    and quite sexy too—
    to be ignored,
    ignored by you.

Heart on the Line

Love is good,
      it is never bad—
      but it will drive you mad!

When it is given to you,
      in dribs and drabs.

Sea of Strangers

In a sea of strangers,
    you've longed to know me.
    Your life spent sailing
    to my shores.

The arms that yearn
    to someday hold me,
    will ache beneath
    the heavy oars.

Please take your time
    and take it slowly;
    as all you do
    will run its course.

And nothing else
    can take what only—
    was always meant
    as solely yours.

Art and Books

Without a doubt,
    I must read,
    all the books
    I've read about.

See the artworks
    hung on hooks,
    that I have only,
    seen in books.

A Voyage

To be guided
    nor misguided
    in love,
    nor brokenhearted.

But to sail in waters—
    uncharted.

A Thank-You Note

You have said
    all the things
    I need to hear
    before I knew
    I needed to hear them.

To be unafraid
    of all the things
    I used to fear,
    before I knew
    I shouldn't fear them.

An Endearing Trait

The scatterbrain,
    is a little like,
        the patter of rain.

Neither here,
    nor there,
        but everywhere.

His Word

I am not,
    just a notch
    on his belt.

What he feels for me,
    he's never felt.

I am a word
    he has heard
    but has never seen
    for himself.

Yet he wants to know,
    how that word
    is spelt.

A Well-Dressed Man

His charm
　　will disarm;
　　his smile,
　　in style;
　　his fashion,
　　in passion;
　　his words,
　　his flirt,
　　his tie
　　from his shirt,
　　to my wrists—
　　his kiss!
　　his kiss!
　　his kiss!

A Stranger

There is a love I reminisce,
    like a seed
      I've never sown.

Of lips that I am yet to kiss,
    and eyes
      not met my own.

Hands that wrap around my wrists,
    and arms
      that feel like home.

I wonder how it is I miss,
    these things
      I've never known.

WALLFLOWER

Shrinking in a corner,
    pressed into the wall;
    do they know I'm present,
    am I here at all?

Is there a written rule book,
    that tells you how to be—
    all the right things to talk about—
    that everyone has but me?

Slowly I am withering—
    a flower deprived of sun;
    longing to belong to—
    somewhere or someone.

A Rollercoaster

You will find him in
    my highs and lows;
    in my mind,
    he'll to and fro.

He's the tallest person,
    that I know—
    and so he keeps me,
    on my toes.

His Cause and Effect

He makes me turn,
    he makes me toss;
    his words mean mine
    are at a loss.

He makes me blush!

He makes me want
    to brush and floss.

LOST AND FOUND

A sunken chest,
 on the ocean ground,
 to never be found
 was where he found me.

There he stirred,
 my every thought,
 my every word,
 so gently, so profoundly.

Now I am kept,
 from dreams I dreamt,
 when once I slept,
 so soundly.

Afraid to Love

I turn away
    and close my heart—
    to the promise of love
    that is luring.

For the past has taught
    to not be caught,
    in what is not
    worth pursuing—

To never do
    the things I've done
    that once had led
    to my undoing.

The Wanderer

What is she like?
    I was told—
    she is a
    melancholy soul.

She is like
    the sun to night;
    a momentary gold.

A star when dimmed
    by dawning light;
    the flicker of
    a candle blown.

A lonely kite
    lost in flight—
    someone once
    had flown.

Part 2
THE CIRCUS OF SORROWS

Circus Town

From a city so bright
    to a strange little town;
    on a carousel spinning,
    around and around.

The dizzying height,
    of the stars from the ground.

The world all alight—
    with his sights, his sounds.

A Timeline

You and I
    against a rule,
    set for us by time.

A marker drawn
    to show our end,
    etched into its line.

The briefest moment
    shared with you—
    the longest
    on my mind.

In Two Parts

You come and go so easily,
    your life is as you knew—
    while mine is split in two.

How I envy so the half of me,
    who lived before love's due,
    who was yet to know of you.

A Bad Day

When thoughts of all but one,
    are those I am keeping.

When sore though there is none,
    for whom I am weeping.

A curtain drawn before the sun,
    and I wish to go on sleeping.

Rogue Planets

As a kid, I would count backwards from ten and imagine at one, there would be an explosion—perhaps caused by a rogue planet crashing into Earth or some other major catastrophe. When nothing happened, I'd feel relieved and at the same time, a little disappointed.

I think of you at ten; the first time I saw you. Your smile at nine and how it lit up something inside me I had thought long dead. Your lips at eight pressed against mine and at seven, your warm breath in my ear and your hands everywhere. You tell me you love me at six and at five we have our first real fight. At four we have our second and three, our third. At two you tell me you can't go on any longer and then at one, you ask me to stay.

And I am relieved, so relieved—and a little disappointed.

CLOSURE

Like time suspended,
    a wound unmended—
    you and I.

We had no ending,
    no said good-bye.

For all my life,
    I'll wonder why.

A Question

It was a question I had worn on my lips for days—like a loose thread on my favorite sweater I couldn't resist pulling—despite knowing it could all unravel around me.

"Do you love me?" I ask.

In your hesitation I found my answer.

A Way Out

Do you know what it is like,
    to lie in bed awake;
    with thoughts to haunt
    you every night,
    of all your past mistakes.

Knowing sleep will set it right—
    if you were not to wake.

Lost Things

Do you know when you've lost something—like your favorite T-shirt or a set of keys—and while looking for it, you come across something else you once missed but have long since forgotten? Well whatever it was, there was a point where you decided to stop searching, maybe because it was no longer required or a new replacement was found. It is almost as if it never existed in the first place—until that moment of rediscovery, a flash of recognition.

Everyone has one—an inventory of lost things waiting to be found. Yearning to be acknowledged for the worth they once held in your life.

I think this is where I belong—among all your other lost things. A crumpled note at the bottom of a drawer or an old photograph pressed between the pages of a book. I hope someday you will find me and remember what I once meant to you.

A Betrayal

I cannot undo
    what I have done;
    I can't un-sing
    a song that's sung.

And the saddest thing
    about my regret—

I can't forgive me,
    and you can't forget.

After You

If I wrote it in a book,
    could I shelve it?

If I told of what you took,
    would that help it?

If I will it,
    can I un-feel it,
    now I've felt it?

A Reverie

A dusty room,
    a window chair,
    unseeing eyes
    that gaze into
    the montage of
    a love affair.

A carousel
    of memories,
    spinning round
    into a blur.

Her mind is now
    a fairground ride—
    she wonders if
    you think of her.

Letting Him Go

There is a particular kind of suffering to be experienced when you love something greater than yourself. A tender sacrifice.

Like the pained silence felt in the lost song of a mermaid; or the bent and broken feet of a dancing ballerina. It is in every considered step I am taking in the opposite direction of you.

The Things We Hide

And so,
    I have put away
    the photographs,
    every trace of you
    I know.

The things that seem
    to matter less,
    are the ones
    we put on show.

Love Lost

There is one who you belong to,
 whose love—there is no song for.
 And though you know it's wrongful,
 there is someone else you long for.

Your heart was once a vessel,
 it was filled up to the brim;
 until the day he left you,
 now everything sings of him.

Of the two who came to love you,
 to one, your heart you gave.
 He lives in stars above you—
 in the love who came and stayed.

TIME TRAVELERS

In all our wrongs,
    I want to write him,
    in a time where
    I can find him.

Before the tears
    that tore us.

When our history was
    before us.

A Small Consolation

Everything that we once were,
    is now a sad and lonely verse.

When once I had so much to say,
    I am now bereft of words.

Sometimes it is the order of things,
    that make them seem much worse.

It's not as if you would have stayed,
    if I hadn't left you first.

An Impossible Task

To try
    or untry
    to forget you not,
    may be related
    somewhat—

To tying,
    then trying
    to untie,
    a complicated
    knot.

The Keeper

You were like a dream,
    I wish I hadn't
    slept through.

Within it I fell deeper,
    than your heart would
    care to let you.

I thought you were a keeper,
    I wish I could
    have kept you.

SAD SONGS

Once there was a boy who couldn't speak but owned a music box that held every song in all the world. One day he met a girl who had never heard a single melody in her entire life and so he played her his favorite song. He watched while her face lit up with wonder as the music filled the sky and the poetry of lyrics moved her in a way she had never felt before.

He would play his songs for her day after day and she would sit by him quietly—never seeming to mind that he could only speak to her through song. She loved everything he played for her, but of them all—she loved the sad songs best. So he began to play them more and more until eventually, sad songs were all she would hear.

One day, he noticed it had been a very long time since her last smile. When he asked her why, she took both his hands in hers and kissed them warmly. She thanked him for his gift of music and poetry but above all else—for showing her sadness because she had known neither of these things before him. But it was now time for her to go away—to find someone who could show her what happiness was.

. . . .

Do you remember the song that was playing the night we met? No, but I remember every song I have heard since you left.

JEALOUSY

It was the way
    you spoke about her.

With animosity, regret, disdain
    and underneath it all—
      just a hint of pride.

Waking without You

Every song that sings of him,
    from every heart
      heard breaking.

I sing along in dreams of him,
    I cling to—
      when I start waking.

That Day

I remember our highs in hues,
    like the color of his eyes
    as the sun was setting;
    the pale of his hands in mine,
    and the blue of his smile.

I remember our sorrows in shades,
    like the gray of the shadows,
    which loomed that day,
    and the white in his lie
    when he promised to stay.

The Girl He Loves

There was a man who I once knew,
    for me there was no other.
    The closer to loving me he grew,
    the more he would grow further.

I tried to love him as his friend,
    then to love him as his lover;
    but he never loved me in the end—
    his heart was for another.

A Lover's Past

The turbulent turns
    and the tides
      that twist them.

When what they once were,
    was how she
      had wished them.

And all the joys he brought her,
    how she could
      list them.

In time she will learn,
    not to
      miss them.

Beauty's Curse

Her bow is drawn
    to worlds of dark;
    where arrows spring
    and miss their mark.

She'll turn their heads—
    but not their hearts.

Dead Butterflies

I sometimes think about the fragility of glass—of broken shards tearing against soft skin. When in truth, it is the transparency that kills you. The pain of seeing through to something you can never quite touch.

For years I've kept you in secret, behind a glass screen. I've watched helplessly as day after day, your new girlfriend becomes your wife and then later, the mother of your children. Then realizing the irony in thinking you were the one under glass when in fact it has been me—a pinned butterfly—static and unmoving, watching while your other life unfolds.

WISHFUL THINKING

You say that you are over me,
 my heart—
 it skips,
 it sinks.

I see you now with someone new,
 I stare,
 I stare,
 I blink.

Someday I'll be over you,
 I know,
 I know—
 I think.

A Heavy Heart

All you have done,
    I had hoped to pardon.

When the death of love
    was slow for me—
    for you was sudden.

Now the years go by,
    and my heart
    has hardened.

Saving You

The darkness takes him over,
 the sickness pulls him in;
 his eyes—a blown-out candle;
 I wish to go with him.

Sometimes I see a flicker—
 a light that shone from them;
 I hold him to me tightly,
 before he's gone again.

An Answer

To choose from
    there were many;
    among them,
    there were some.

And of those I loved you,
    more than any—
    but not as much
    as one.

Swan Song

Her heart is played
   like well-worn strings;
   in her eyes,
   the sadness sings—
   of one who was destined
   for better things.

Part 3
LOVE

First Love

Before I fell
    in love with words,
    with setting skies
    and singing birds—
    it was you I fell
    in love with first.

He and I

When words run dry,
    he does not try,
    nor do I.

We are on par.

He just is,
    I just am,
    and we just are.

Sundays with Michael

I hold my breath and count to ten,
    I stand and sit, then stand again.
    I cross and then uncross my legs,
    the planes are flying overhead.

The dial turns with every twist,
    around the watch, around his wrist.
    Resting there with pen in hand,
    who could ever understand?

The way he writes of all I dream,
    things kind yet cruel and in-between,
    where underneath those twisted trees,
    a pretty girl fallen to her knees.

Who could know the world we've spun?
    I shrug my shoulders and hold my tongue.
    I hold my breath and count to ten,
    I stand and sit, then stand again.

Mornings with You

I slowly wake
    as day is dawning,
    to fingertips
    and lips imploring.

The sheets against my skin,
    he says,
    like wrapping paper
    on Christmas morning.

Soul Mates

I don't know how you are so familiar to me—or why it feels less like I am getting to know you and more as though I am remembering who you are. How every smile, every whisper brings me closer to the impossible conclusion that I have known you before, I have loved you before—in another time, a different place—some other existence.

A Fairy Tale

Start of spring;
    heart in bloom;
    our whisperings
    in sunlit rooms.

Summer was felt
    a little more;
    in autumn I
    began to fall.

When winter came
    with all its white,
    you were mine
    to kiss goodnight.

Always

You were you,
    and I was I;
    we were two
    before our time.

I was yours
    before I knew,
    and you have always
    been mine too.

A Dream

As the Earth began spinning faster and faster, we floated upwards, hands locked tightly together, eyes sad and bewildered. We watched as our faces grew younger and realized the Earth was spinning in reverse, moving us backwards in time.

Then we reached a point where I no longer knew who you were and I was grasping the hands of a stranger. But I didn't let go. And neither did you.

. . . .

I had my first dream about you last night.
Really? She smiles. What was it about?
I don't remember exactly, but the whole time I was dreaming, I knew you were mine.

Before There Was You

When I used to look above,
    all I saw was sky;
    and every song
    that I would sing,
    I sung not knowing why.

All I thought and all I felt,
    was only just because,
    never was it ever you—
    until it was all there was.

Beautiful

Your hand reaches for mine.
    We kiss tentatively, passionately
    and then, tenderly.

You brush my hair away from my face.
    "You're beautiful."
    I wrinkle my nose in protest.
    "You are."

ALL OR NOTHING

If you love me
    for what you see,
    only your eyes would be
    in love with me.

If you love me
    for what you've heard,
    then you would love me
    for my words.

If you love
    my heart and mind,
    then you would love me,
    for all that I'm.

But if you don't love
    my every flaw,
    then you mustn't love me—
    not at all.

SOME TIME OUT

The time may not
    be prime for us,
    though you are
    a special person.

We may be just
    two different clocks,
    that do not tock,
    in unison.

Souls

When two souls fall in love, there is nothing else but the yearning to be close to the other. The presence that is felt through a hand held, a voice heard, or a smile seen.

Souls do not have calendars or clocks, nor do they understand the notion of time or distance. They only know it feels right to be with one another.

This is the reason why you miss someone so much when they are not there—even if they are only in the very next room. Your soul only feels their absence—it doesn't realize the separation is temporary.

. . . .

Can I ask you something?
Anything.
Why is it every time we say good night, it feels like good-bye?

Solo Show

He pulls the thick woolen sweater
    up, over my head.

Little sparks of static
    dance across my skin.

Does it hurt? He says, running his hands
    gently over my warm body.

It is your own little fireworks show,
    I whisper.

THE FEAR OF LOSING YOU

Without meaning to,
    he's disarmed me,
    with kisses that soothe
    and alarm me.

In arms that terrify
    and calm me.

Ebb and Flow

She yearns to learn
    how his tide is turned,
    to understand
    each grain of sand,
    he knows.

To move in rhythm,
    with his ebb and flow.

Written in Traffic

A quiet gladness,
    in the busy sadness;
    inside the final tussle,
    of love and its madness.

Its goodness and badness,
    its hustle and bustle.

Angels

It happens like this. One day you meet someone and for some inexplicable reason, you feel more connected to this stranger than anyone else—closer to them than your closest family. Perhaps because this person carries an angel within them—one sent to you for some higher purpose, to teach you an important lesson or to keep you safe during a perilous time. What you must do is trust in them—even if they come hand in hand with pain or suffering—the reason for their presence will become clear in due time.

Though here is a word of warning—you may grow to love this person but remember they are not yours to keep. Their purpose isn't to save you but to show you how to save yourself. And once this is fulfilled, the halo lifts and the angel leaves their body as the person exits your life. They will be a stranger to you once more.

. . . .

It's so dark right now, I can't see any light around me.
That's because the light is coming from you. You can't see it but everyone else can.

GOLDEN CAGE

A bird who hurt her wing,
    now forgotten how to fly.

A song she used to sing,
    but can't remember why.

A breath she caught and kept—
    that left her in a sigh.

It hurts her so to love you,
    but she won't say good-bye.

LOVE LETTERS

Every letter
    that she types,
    every keystroke
    that she strikes—

To spell your name
    again and again—
    is all she ever
    wants to write.

Codependency

There is nothing more nice,
    there is nothing much worser;
    than me as your vice
    and you as my versa.

CANYONS

Rarely do the words *I love you* precede a question mark—but it is a question nonetheless and your answer to mine was the incarnation of a wish—the fulfillment of a promise.

Somewhere between falling in and out of love, the question spilled from our lips over and over—readily answered with greedy hands and ravenous mouths. It was cautiously whispered on rooftops, as we looked down on terrifying heights and cried out under creased, white sheets in breathless admissions.

Towards good-bye, I asked the question, and your reply was a thoughtless echo as I stood, feeling as though I was shouting meaningless words into an empty canyon—just to hear them repeated back.

. . . .

I love you, he says for the first time.
I turn my body to face his. *Say it again.*
He says it over and over again, pulling me beneath him.

A Time Capsule

This is where,
    I began to care,
    where I was befriended.

This is where,
    my soul was bared,
    where all my rules were bended.

This is where,
    a moment we shared,
    was stolen and expended.

Now this is where,
    this is where,
    this is where we've ended—

Index

PART 3 - LOVE 109

About the Author

The work of poet and artist Lang Leav swings between the whimsical and woeful, expressing a complexity beneath its childlike facade.

Lang is a recipient of the Qantas Spirit of Youth Award and a prestigious Churchill Fellowship.

Her artwork is exhibited internationally and she was selected to take part in the landmark Playboy Redux show curated by the Andy Warhol Museum.

She currently lives with her partner and collaborator, Michael, in a little house by the sea.

The Fell Types are digitally reproduced by Igino Marini. www.iginomarini.com

POSTED POEMS

Posted Poems is a unique postal service that allows you to send your favorite Lang Leav poem to anyone, anywhere in the world. All poems are printed on heavyweight art paper and encased in a beautiful string-tie envelope. To send a Posted Poem to someone special visit: langleav.com/postedpoems